Movie Star Pony

Do you love ponies? Be a Pony Pal!

PONY PALS

Movie Star Pony

Jeanne Betancourt

illustrated by Rachel Tonkin

SCHOLASTIC INC.
New York   Toronto   London   Auckland   Sydney
Mexico City   New Delhi   Hong Kong

ISBN 0-439-06492-9

12 11 10 9 8 7 6 5 4 3 2 1   0 1 2 3 4 5 6/0

Printed in Australia

First Scholastic printing, March 2000
Cover and text illustrations by Rachel Tonkin
Typeset in Bookman

Contents

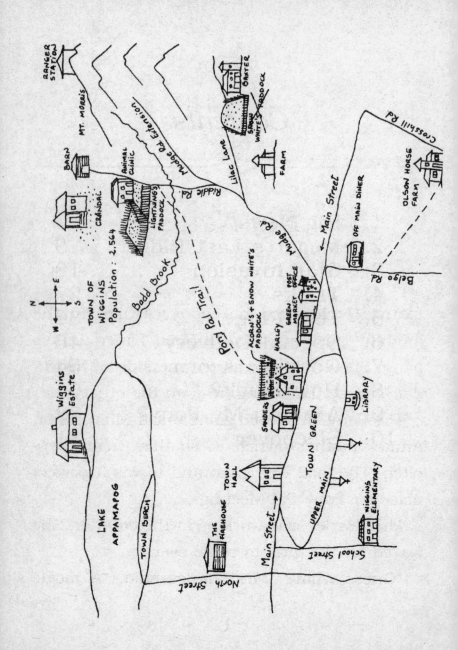

Big News

Anna Harley tied her pony, Acorn, to the hitching post outside Off-Main Diner. Lulu's pony, Snow White, was on one side of Acorn. Pam's pony, Lightning, was on the other side.

The Pony Pals loved going to Off-Main Diner. Anna's mother owned it, so they went there often. The food was great and it was a perfect place for Pony Pal Meetings.

Mrs. Harley was working at the counter. She waved for the girls to come over.

"Guess what?" Mrs. Harley said. "A movie

company is shooting a film in Wiggins. They want to rent my diner for one of the scenes."

"Wow!" exclaimed Lulu.

"Will you be in the movie, Mom?" asked Anna.

"No," she answered. "My customers can't even be in the diner that day. Only actors. I'll have to close it to customers."

"What's the movie about?" asked Lulu.

Mrs. Harley squirted whipped cream on a piece of cake. "I'll tell you in a minute," she said. "But first I have to serve this and take an order."

While Mrs. Harley waited on her customers, the girls made themselves chocolate-cream sodas. They were sitting at the counter drinking them when Mrs. Harley came back.

"The movie is called *Megan's Last Ride*," she told the three girls. "It stars Bette Fleming."

"Bette Fleming is a great actress!" said Anna excitedly. "She's the best."

"She *is* very good," agreed Mrs. Harley. "And she's only eleven years old."

"Remember her in *The Rainbow Kid*?" asked Lulu. "That was such a good movie."

"When the girl died at the end I cried," Anna remembered.

"I wonder what *Megan's Last Ride* is about," said Lulu.

"Maybe the *ride* part is about riding a pony," said Anna.

"It could be a bike ride," suggested Pam. "Or a car ride."

"Or any kind of ride," added Lulu. "Even a roller coaster."

"Maybe they call it the <u>last</u> ride because Megan dies," said Pam.

"I hope it's not as sad as *The Rainbow Kid*," said Anna.

"Do you think we can meet Bette Fleming?" Lulu asked Mrs. Harley. "That'd be fun."

"I don't see why not," she answered. "They'll be shooting in Wiggins for a couple of weeks."

The girls were still talking about the movie when Ms. Wiggins came into the diner.

Ms. Wiggins lived in a mansion on a big estate with a lot of riding trails. She was a special friend of the Pony Pals and loved ponies and horses as much as they did. The Pony Pals could ride on Ms. Wiggins' trails whenever they wanted.

"Hi, everybody," she said as she came up to the group at the counter. "I have some big news."

"So do we," said Anna excitedly. "You go first."

"A man and woman from a movie company stopped by my place today," she began. "They're making a movie in Wiggins and want to rent my house for two weeks—for the lead actors and director."

Anna's mother gave Ms. Wiggins a cup of coffee and a piece of apple pie. "Did you say *yes*?" she asked. "Are you going to rent it to them?"

"I am," Ms. Wiggins answered. She smiled. "They're paying me a lot of money. It will help pay my taxes."

"Where will you live?" asked Pam.

"I can sleep in my art studio on the top floor," she said. "They can use the rest of the house."

Anna told Ms. Wiggins the news about the diner being in the movie, too.

"Do you know what the movie is about?" Lulu asked Ms. Wiggins. "We just know it's called *Megan's Last Ride* and Bette Fleming is in it."

"You girls are going to love it," said Ms. Wiggins. "It's the story of a girl and her pony."

"So *Megan's Last Ride* is about riding a pony," exclaimed Pam.

"Does the girl die at the end?" asked Anna. "Is that why it's called *Megan's* Last *Ride*?"

"I don't know," answered Ms. Wiggins. "They didn't tell me what happens to Megan and her pony."

"Maybe the pony dies," said Anna. "That'd make me cry for sure."

"I have something else to tell you," said Ms. Wiggins.

"What?" asked the Pony Pals in unison.

"The director asked me if there were any riding schools in the area," Ms. Wiggins answered.

"Did you tell them about Pam's mother's riding school?" asked Anna.

"I most certainly did," said Ms. Wiggins. She smiled at Pam. "They were going to call your mother right away. They wanted to meet with her this afternoon."

"What do they need a riding school for?" asked Lulu.

"I don't know," answered Ms. Wiggins. "They didn't say."

"Maybe they need a stable for the star pony," suggested Pam.

"That's not it," said Ms. Wiggins. "The pony is staying in my barn."

"Wow! I want to see that pony," said Lulu. "A movie star pony. That'll be so much fun."

"Let's go to Pam's," Anna said as she jumped off the stool. "If we hurry, the movie people might still be there."

"And we can find out why they need a riding school," said Pam.

"And what happens to Megan and the pony in the movie," added Anna.

The girls cleared the counter, said goodbye to Ms. Wiggins and Mrs. Harley and ran outside to their ponies.

Pam untied Lightning's rope, "Maybe Bette needs riding lessons," she said.

"If she took lessons from Pam's mother we'd meet her for sure," said Anna as she mounted Acorn.

"It'd be so great if your barns are in the movie, Pam," said Lulu.

Anna turned Acorn to face Belgo Road.

"Let's go, Acorn," she said. "We're going to find out all about *Megan's Last Ride* and the movie star pony."

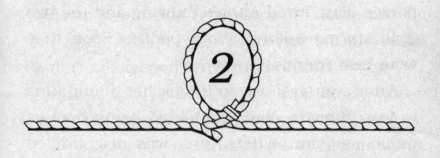

Megan's Last Ride

Pam took the lead on Riddle Road. Anna followed, and Lulu took up the rear. I hope those movie people are still at Pam's, thought Anna.

Pam moved Lightning into a trot. Anna noticed Pam's perfect riding posture and the smooth way she posted. Pam's mother was a riding teacher and her father was a veterinarian, so Pam had been riding ponies all her life.

Anna met Pam Crandal on the first day of

kindergarten. Anna was drawing a picture of ponies. Pam loved Anna's drawing and the two girls started talking about ponies. Soon they were best friends.

Anna was dyslexic so it took her a long time to learn how to read. She didn't like school as much as Pam. When Anna was discouraged about her grades, Pam reminded her that she was a great artist.

Anna remembered the first time she went to the Crandals' and saw all the horses and ponies. She took her first riding lesson that day. She still loved going to the Crandals'. And she loved having Pam as her oldest, best friend.

Anna turned in the saddle to check on Lulu and Snow White. The white pony trotted proudly behind Acorn, and Lulu had a big grin on her face. Lulu loves ponies as much as Pam and I do, thought Anna.

Lulu Sanders was Anna's and Pam's new, best friend. They met Lulu when she moved to Wiggins after her tenth birthday.

Lulu's mother died when she was three years old. Her father was a naturalist who traveled all over the world studying wild animals. For a long time Lulu traveled with her father on his business trips. Now she was living with her grandmother in Wiggins.

Wiggins is a great place to live, thought Anna. I hope that Bette Fleming likes it.

"They're here!" Pam shouted. Anna noticed a big, fancy car parked in the driveway. A man and woman were talking to Mrs. Crandal near the barn.

Pam waved to her mother and the girls rode over to her.

"These are the wonderful ponies we saw outside the diner!" exclaimed the woman.

"The diner belongs to Anna's mother," Pam explained.

"I'm Anna," said Anna proudly.

Mrs. Crandal introduced Lulu and Pam to the man and woman. They were Nancy Cross, the director of *Megan's Last Ride*, and Roger Levine, the producer of the movie.

"We're friends of Ms. Wiggins," added Lulu. "She told us you might be here."

"Are you going to be in the movie, Mrs. Crandal?" asked Anna.

"Not me," answered Mrs. Crandal. "But our old barn will be."

"We're going to film a scene there," explained Ms. Cross. "With a girl and her pony."

"The girl is Bette Fleming," said Lulu.

"And the movie is called *Megan's Last Ride*," added Pam. "But that's all we know."

"What's the story?" asked Anna. "Please tell us."

"I'd like to hear it, too," said Mrs. Crandal.

"Bette Fleming plays Megan Ritter," began Ms. Cross. "Her family owns a big farm. At the beginning of the story they are having money problems. Then a freak summer hailstorm destroys their apple crop. After that, they know they will have to sell the farm and move to the city for jobs."

"What about the pony?" asked Anna.

"That would be Mars—Megan's pony," said Mr. Levine. "Megan and Mars are best friends."

"Like us and our ponies," said Lulu.

"Mars and Megan understand one another very well," added Ms. Cross. "It's almost as if they can read one another's minds. They have a special psychic connection."

Anna put an arm around Acorn's neck. That's how I feel about Acorn, she thought.

"Anyway," continued Ms. Cross, "Megan's parents both find jobs in the city. They tell Megan they are moving to an apartment and she has to sell Mars. Of course, Megan is very sad and cries a lot."

"I would, too," said Anna. "If that happened to me."

"Megan's parents sell Mars to a local riding school," said Mr. Levine. He smiled at Pam.

"We're filming the goodbye scene between Megan and Mars in your barn."

"That's so sad," said Anna. "Bette Fleming's movies always have sad endings."

"But that's not the end of the movie," said Ms. Cross. "After saying goodbye to Mars and moving to the city, Megan becomes very sick. No one knows what is wrong with her."

"She's sick because she misses Mars so much," said Lulu.

"Yes," agreed Ms. Cross. "Mars misses Meagan, too. And even though he's a hundred miles away, he senses that something is wrong. So he runs away from the school to find Megan."

"A hundred miles!" exclaimed Pam. "How will he know the way?"

"He's a special pony," said Mr. Levine. "But you're right. It's a very difficult journey."

"Meanwhile Megan is so sick," said Ms. Cross. "Her parents are afraid that she will die."

"Does Mars make it before Megan dies?" asked Anna.

"One night," Ms. Cross continued, "Megan hears Mars' whinny. Her parents think she is imagining it. But when they look out the window they see Mars on the street."

"Megan's mother and father sneak Mars into the apartment building," said Mr. Levine. "Megan and Mars are reunited. For that night, Mars stays on the little terrace outside Megan's room. The next morning Megan's fever is gone. Her parents say they will buy Mars back. They'll board him at a stable near the city. Megan and Mars will never be separated again."

"That's a great story," said Anna.

"I think I'd get sick if I had to sell Snow White," said Lulu.

"What does Mars look like?" asked Pam.

"He's a beautiful pony," answered Ms. Cross. She opened her briefcase. "I have a photo I can show you."

Ms. Cross showed the girls and Mrs. Crandal

a photo of a sleek, black pony. Everyone agreed that he was handsome.

That night the Pony Pals had a barn sleepover in the Crandals' hayloft. At nine-thirty they turned off the lights and slipped into their sleeping bags.

"I can't wait to meet Bette and Mars," said Anna.

"Do you think Bette will be a good rider?" asked Lulu.

"She has to be," answered Pam. "If she's going to ride Mars in a movie."

"Maybe she'll ride with us some time," said Anna. "Like on her day off. It would be fun to ride with a movie star."

Anna looked out at the starlit sky. In ten more days Bette Fleming and Mars the Movie Star Pony were coming to Wiggins.

She couldn't wait.

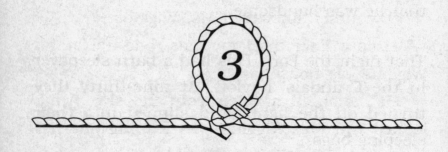

Star Invasion

Ten days later Ms. Wiggins phoned Anna. "Well, they're here," she announced. "Bette Fleming, her mother, three other actors and Nancy Cross moved into my house late yesterday. They start shooting the film tomorrow."

"Is Bette nice?" asked Anna. "Is she a good rider?"

"She seems nice," answered Ms. Wiggins. "But I haven't seen her ride yet. Do you want to come over and meet her this afternoon?"

"Can I bring Pam and Lulu?" asked Anna.

"Of course," answered Ms. Wiggins.

An hour later the Pony Pals rode up to Ms. Wiggins' big house.

"Hi," shouted a voice from the sky. Anna looked up. Ms. Wiggins was leaning out her studio window. "I'll be right down."

Just then a girl walked out of the house. It was Bette Fleming. She looked very surprised to see three girls and their ponies.

"Hi," said Pam as she dismounted. "I'm Pam Crandal. Ms. Wiggins said to come over."

Lulu and Anna dismounted and introduced themselves, too. By then Ms. Wiggins had joined them.

"I invited these girls over to meet you," Ms. Wiggins explained to Bette. "I thought it would be fun for you to meet some local kids."

"Oh," said Bette in a bored voice. She walked over to Acorn and patted his head. "He's cute," she said. "What's his name?"

19

Anna told Bette, then she introduced the other ponies.

Bette didn't pay any attention to Lightning, Snow White *or* the Pony Pals. She only looked at Acorn.

"I used to ride a pony just like you," Bette told Acorn.

"Where's Mars?" asked Anna.

"I don't know," answered Bette.

"He arrived this morning," Ms. Wiggins said. "I think he's in the barn with his trainer."

"Let's go and see him," suggested Lulu. She turned to Bette. "Okay?"

"Sure," answered Bette.

The four girls went to the barn together. Anna wanted to ask Bette what it was like to be a movie star. But she felt too shy.

The Pony Pals tied their ponies to the hitching post. Just then a man came out of the barn. He was leading a pony saddled for riding. Anna

thought it was the shiniest, blackest, sleekest pony she'd ever seen.

"Hi, there," said the man.

"You must be Carson," said Bette.

"And you're Miss Fleming," said the man. He took off his cap. "It's a pleasure to meet you, Miss Fleming."

Bette didn't bother to introduce the Pony Pals to Carson. They had to do that themselves.

"Are you going to ride Mars?" Lulu asked Carson.

"Miss Fleming's going to ride him," Carson answered. He patted Mars on the head and smiled at Bette. "You two have to get to know one another. You'll be working together on this movie."

"Can they go on a trail ride with us?" Pam asked the horse trainer.

"Ms. Wiggins has some terrific trails," Lulu told Bette. "That's how we got here."

"Fine with me," said Carson. "But first you

have to ride in the ring, Bette. I need to see what kind of rider you are."

"I don't want to ride today," Bette said.

"You have to ride today, Bette," said a voice behind Anna.

Anna turned and saw Ms. Cross.

"We start shooting tomorrow," added Ms. Cross.

"I'll ride in the ring," Bette told Ms. Cross and Carson. "But I'm not going on a trail ride with those girls." Bette looked around at the Pony Pals. "And I don't want them watching me ride, either," she added in a snobby voice.

The Pony Pals exchanged a glance. They were all surprised that Bette was being so rude to them.

"Guess we'd better go," Pam said.

The Pony Pals said goodbye to Bette, Ms. Cross and Carson.

Bette smiled when she said goodbye. Anna thought it was a phony smile.

"She was so rude to us," whispered Pam as

the three friends walked over to the hitching post.

"I don't like her," said Lulu as she untied Snow White.

"Me either," added Anna. She swung up onto Acorn. "I don't care if she is a movie star."

The Pony Pals rode onto the trail. They kept their ponies at a walk so they could still talk about Bette.

"I'd like to see how she rides," said Pam.

"Maybe she doesn't even know how," suggested Anna.

Lulu suddenly halted Snow White. "There's one way to find out," she told the others.

Anna pulled Acorn up beside Snow White. "How?" she asked Lulu.

"Spying," suggested Lulu with a grin.

"Let's," agreed Anna.

"Good idea," added Pam.

Lulu patted her saddle bag. "I even have my binoculars," she said.

"Perfect," said Anna.

24

They turned their ponies around and headed back to Ms. Wiggins' place.

Before they reached the end of the trail they stopped and dismounted. "I'll stay with the ponies," Pam suggested. "You two go and spy."

Anna followed Lulu to the edge of the woods. Lulu pointed to a clump of bushes between some tall pine trees. She crouched down and ran quickly over to the bushes. Anna followed her.

Anna looked between the branches. She had a perfect view of the corral. Bette was sitting on Mars, but they weren't moving.

"Okay," said Carson. "Let's try that again. Walk around the ring then halt. Remember to keep your heels down."

Lulu and Anna exchanged a glance. Bette was having trouble doing something very easy. Walking and halting were the first thing you learned when you rode a pony.

Lulu handed the binoculars to Anna.

Through them Anna saw Bette in close up. Anna thought Bette looked unhappy and a little frightened of Mars.

If Bette can't ride, thought Anna, how can she be in a big movie about a girl and her pony?

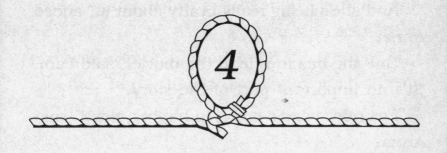

Tricks

Anna watched Bette walk Mars forward. When she tried to make him halt, Mars trotted instead. Bette finally pulled him to a halt.

"I hate this pony!" Bette shouted as she jumped off the pony. "And I'm not going to ride him!"

"She's a terrible rider," Anna whispered to Lulu.

"Let's go and tell Pam," Lulu whispered back.

The two friends ran back to Pam and the ponies.

"Bette can't ride!" Lulu told Pam.

"And she's being really bratty about it," added Anna.

"But she has to ride in the movie," said Pam. "It's an important part of the story."

"I wonder what's going to happen next," said Anna.

"Let's ride over there and find out," suggested Lulu.

"We'll pretend we're riding back that way," said Pam.

"To reach the other trail," added Anna.

The three girls mounted their ponies and rode out of the woods. Bette was standing by the fence with Carson and Ms. Cross. Mars stood quietly beside Carson.

When Bette saw the Pony Pals she waved to them.

"We're just passing through," Pam shouted.

"Come over," Bette called in a friendly voice.

Lulu and Anna exchanged a surprised look. Why was Bette suddenly being nice to them?

The Pony Pals rode up to the corral fence.

"Hi," said Bette.

"I can bring in another pony," Anna heard Carson tell Ms. Cross. "But it will take me a day to get him here."

"And what if Bette can't ride that pony," said Ms. Cross. "We need her to ride in this movie."

"I know how to ride," insisted Bette.

"Then prove it," said Ms. Cross. "Ride Mars for us."

"No!" said Bette.

"You told me you knew how to ride when we hired you," Ms. Cross told Bette. "Now it seems you can't."

"I can!" insisted Bette. She put a hand on Acorn's neck. He nuzzled her sympathetically. "I'll show you on this pony."

"Acorn?" exclaimed Anna.

Ms. Cross looked over at Anna. "Could Bette ride your pony around the ring a couple of times?" she asked. "I need to see her ride."

"Sure," said Anna. "That's okay."

Anna slid off Acorn. Bette took the reins and grinned at Anna. "Thanks," she said. She gave the reins a little tug. "Come on Acorn, honey."

Acorn whinnied happily as he followed Bette into the ring.

Anna leaned against the rail to watch. She felt nervous. She didn't usually let strangers ride her pony.

Bette easily swung herself into the saddle and sat tall.

"She has good posture," Pam whispered to Lulu and Anna.

"Okay, Bette," Carson called out. "Walk him once around the ring. When you pass me, move him into a trot."

Bette and Acorn followed Carson's directions perfectly.

"Canter," Carson called out. "Now!" Acorn instantly moved into a smooth canter.

"She *is* a good rider!" said Lulu.

"Thank goodness," sighed Ms. Cross.

"Why'd she ride Mars so badly?" asked Anna.

30

"She made up her mind she didn't like him," answered Ms. Cross. "Bette Fleming can be very stubborn."

After cantering twice around the ring, Bette pulled Acorn to a halt in front of her audience.

"Well done," said Carson.

Bette smiled proudly. "I know how to jump, too," she bragged.

Carson patted Acorn on the head and turned to Anna. "He's a nice little pony. Thanks for letting her ride him."

"You're welcome," said Anna.

"So you *can* ride, Bette," said Ms. Cross. "Why didn't you ride Mars like that."

"I told you," said Bette. "I don't like him and he doesn't like me."

"Mars is trained to like everyone," said Carson. "But never mind. I'll send for another pony. He'll be here tomorrow."

Bette leaned over and scratched the top of Acorn's head. "I like Acorn. I want him to be my pony in the movie."

Anna couldn't believe her ears. Bette wanted Acorn to star in the movie with her!

"You want what!" exclaimed Carson.

"Don't be ridiculous, Bette," said Ms. Cross.

Anna noticed that Carson's face was getting red. He was losing his patience with Bette.

"Listen to me, young lady," Carson said. "This is a movie. We need to work with a highly trained pony—a pony that can follow directions, do tricks and isn't afraid of lights and crowds."

"Acorn knows lots of tricks," said Pam.

"He was in a circus," added Lulu. "He did great."

"Acorn's not afraid of anything," said Anna proudly. "And he loves crowds."

"Great," said Ms. Cross. "Let's try him out."

"Yes!" exclaimed Bette.

"What kind of tricks would he have to do?" asked Anna. "I don't want him to do anything that's dangerous."

Carson held up his hands. "Wait a minute

here," he said. He turned to Ms. Cross. "Are you serious?" he asked. "Acorn is a little backyard Shetland pony. He can't star in a movie. You need a highly trained pony for that."

"Bette likes Acorn and can ride him," said Ms. Cross. "That's important, too. He's also very cute. People would love to see him in a movie."

"I train ponies and horses for performance," Carson said. "But not in one day. This little pony cannot do what you need."

"At least try him," Ms. Cross said.

"I suppose I could test him," said Carson. "But you'll see I'm right."

Carson took Acorn to the middle of the ring.

Bette stood at the fence between Ms. Cross and Anna.

Anna noticed that Bette's fingers were crossed. She knew that Bette was wishing with all her heart that Acorn would pass the test.

Anna didn't know what she wished for. She wanted everyone to know that Acorn was a special pony. But did she want this awful girl riding him?

Test Ride

"Anna, would you ride Acorn for me, please?" Carson said.

"I'll do it," shouted Bette.

"I want to see how he responds to Anna," Carson told her. "Anna knows what he can do."

"Show him how Acorn can be ridden with voice commands," Pam whispered to Anna.

Anna ran into the ring and swung up on Acorn. She held the reins loosely and directed him to walk, trot and canter using voice commands. When she said, "Whoa," he stopped immediately.

Everyone clapped.

"He can be in the movie," shouted Bette. "Now let me ride him."

"Not so fast," Carson said. "Everyone come into the ring. While Anna rides I want the rest of you to make noise. A lot of noise. Shout. Whistle. Stomp your feet. Wave your arms, too. I want to see how steady he is."

Anna did a walk, trot, and canter around the noisy corral. Acorn didn't even look at the noisemakers and kept steady to his circles.

After three complete turns, Carson signaled Anna and the noisemakers to stop. Anna pulled Acorn to a halt. Ms. Cross and the girls quietened down. Carson grabbed Acorn by the reins and told Anna to dismount.

"I'm taking him into the big field," he said. "There are a few things I want to test out in the open."

"Do you want me to come with you?" asked Anna.

"Me, too," said Bette.

"I need to be alone with him," Carson said.

"You girls can go to the house and have a snack," suggested Ms. Cross.

"No, thanks," said Anna. "I'm going to wait here."

"Me, too," said Bette.

Ms. Cross and the four girls sat on the corral fence. In the distance Carson worked with Acorn.

Lulu took her binoculars out of her pocket. She reached past Bette to hand them to Anna.

"Thanks," said Bette as she grabbed the binoculars from Lulu.

Lulu and Anna exchanged a glance. Neither of them liked Bette.

Bette looked through the binoculars and told the others what was happening. "Carson's walking in circles," she said. "Acorn's following him. When Carson stops, Acorn stops."

Bette didn't hand the binoculars over to Anna until Acorn and Carson were on their way back.

"You girls were right," Carson said when he reached them. "Acorn will be just fine in the movie."

Anna felt proud of her pony. She jumped off the fence to give him a big hug. But Bette reached Acorn first.

Acorn whinnied happily as if to say, "I was wonderful!"

Ms. Cross turned to Anna. "Congratulations," she said. "Your pony is going to be a movie star."

Anna felt her stomach turn over. Did she want Acorn to be in a movie with a girl like Bette Fleming? She gave Pam a desperate look.

"I . . . ah," Anna started to say. "I need to talk to my Pony Pals about this."

"Fine," said Ms. Cross. "Bette and I will meet you at the house."

"I'm staying with Acorn," said Bette.

Anna took Acorn's reins. "He's had a big

workout," she said. "I'm going to cool him down."

Bette pouted. "Then I'll wait here," she said. "And watch you."

"I'll take care of him," Carson told Anna. "He needs to get used to me."

Anna watched Carson lead Acorn into the barn.

Pam pulled on Anna's hand. "Come on," she said. "We'll go behind the barn for our meeting."

"Where we can be private," added Lulu.

The three friends stood in a circle behind the barn.

"I don't know what to do," Anna told Pam and Lulu. "I don't like Bette. But Acorn might like being in a movie."

"He'd have fun," said Lulu. "And he'd learn new tricks."

"They'll pay him, too," said Pam. "Maybe enough money to pay for a new pony shed."

"Everyone will see what a great pony he is,"

added Lulu. "He'll be like the horse who played Black Beauty in the movie."

"I'll miss him," said Anna sadly.

"It's only for two weeks," said Pam.

"Besides," added Lulu, "you'll have him home at night."

"Maybe I could bring him back and forth to work," said Anna. "I didn't think of that. I could ride him to the set. If he's not too tired, I'll ride him home, too."

"You can watch him being a movie star," said Pam.

"We can all watch," said Lulu excitedly. "It's going to be so much fun."

The Pony Pals went around to the front of the barn. Bette was sitting on the fence waiting for them.

"Can Acorn be in the movie?" she asked Anna.

"Yes," Anna said.

"Yeah!" shouted Bette. She jumped off the fence and ran ahead of them to the house.

When the Pony Pals reached the house, Ms. Cross was waiting for them on the porch.

"I heard the good news," she said. She smiled at Anna. "Shall I do the business arrangements with your mother?"

"Yes," agreed Anna. "What time do you want Acorn in the mornings?"

"We start pretty early," answered Ms. Cross. "But you don't have to worry about that. He'll already be here."

"He can still live with me," said Anna. "I'll bring him here every day—as early as you want. I'll bring him home, too. Really, it's no trouble."

"We need to keep him here all the time, Anna," said Ms. Cross. "I'm sure that's what Carson wants."

"Me, too," said Bette. "I'm going to take care of him."

"Can Anna stay here, too?" asked Pam.

"I can sleep in the barn," said Anna.

"We'll stay with her sometimes," added Lulu. "We have barn sleepovers all the time."

"I guess that's all right," said Ms. Cross. "If Ms. Wiggins doesn't mind."

"She won't mind," said Anna. This will be fun, she thought. I'll be with Acorn all day and all night. The only bad part is Bette.

Carson came onto the porch. "Acorn and Mars are getting along just fine," he said.

"Acorn likes other ponies," said Anna.

"So it's all settled," said Carson with a smile. "Acorn's in the movie."

Anna nodded.

"But you can't stay with him, Anna," said Bette. "Acorn has to get used to me. If you're here he will be confused."

"He's my pony," said Anna. "I'll help."

"He's *my* pony for the movie," said Bette. She turned to Ms. Cross. "Isn't he?"

"In a way, yes," answered Ms. Cross. "I'm sorry, Anna. It's better if you just leave Acorn with us. We'll take good care of him."

"It's just for two weeks," Lulu told Anna.

"Then he'll be a star in a movie," added Pam.

"You can ride one of my Mom's school ponies for the two weeks."

Anna looked towards the field. Acorn and Mars were happily grazing side by side. She remembered how much fun Acorn had had, being in the circus. He'd probably like being in a movie, too.

"Okay," said Anna.

"Yeah!" shouted Bette as she ran from the porch.

"Don't worry about Acorn, Anna," Ms. Cross told Anna. "He's going to be fine."

"I know," answered Anna. But she felt sad.

She looked over to the field again. Bette was heading in Acorn's direction. Anna watched her run over to Acorn and give him a big hug.

Anna wondered if she'd made a big mistake.

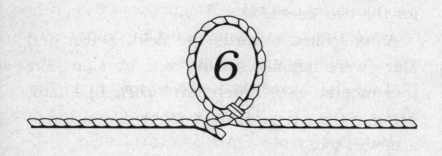

Special Delivery

The Pony Pals sat in their favorite booth at Off-Main diner. Anna poked at her blueberry pancakes with the fork.

"Aren't you hungry?" asked Lulu.

"I miss Acorn," said Anna sadly. "I haven't seen him in nine days. I hope he's okay."

"If he wasn't okay, they'd call you," said Pam.

"I guess," said Anna.

Lulu pointed out the window. "Look," she said. "Ms. Wiggins is here. Maybe she can tell you about Acorn."

46

Anna rapped on the window to get Ms. Wiggins' attention. Ms. Wiggins waved to her. When Ms. Wiggins came into the diner she walked right over to the girls.

Anna slid over to make room for her in the booth.

"How is everyone?" Ms. Wiggins asked.

"Anna misses Acorn," said Lulu.

Ms. Wiggins put an arm around Anna's shoulder and gave her a squeeze. "I bet you do," she said. "But you should be proud of Acorn, Anna," she said. "He's doing so well. Everyone on the set loves him. He's getting a lot of attention."

"I hope they don't spoil him," said Anna.

"Carson is an experienced horse trainer," Ms. Wiggins told her. "He won't let Acorn be spoiled."

"What about Bette?" asked Pam. "Is she riding him all right."

"Bette's doing fine," answered Ms. Wiggins. "Today they're filming her grooming him. Then they'll do some trail riding shots." Ms. Wiggins

47

smiled at Pam. "Tomorrow they're shooting the goodbye scene in your barn."

"I wish I could see that," said Lulu.

"Me, too," said Anna. "But I can't go near Acorn. It's awful."

Lulu asked Ms. Wiggins if she wanted something to eat or drink.

"No, thanks," Ms. Wiggins said as she slid out of the booth. "I stopped because I saw the ponies out front." She patted Anna on the head. "I wanted to tell Anna that Acorn is just fine," she said.

"I'm never going to let other people take care of him again," Anna told Ms. Wiggins. "Never."

Ms. Wiggins said goodbye and left the diner.

Pam leaned forward. "I have the best idea," she whispered excitedly.

"What?" asked Lulu.

"I know where they're going to shoot that scene tomorrow," Pam answered.

"We all know that," said Lulu. "In the barn."

"But I know *where* in the barn," Pam told them. "My mom told me."

"Where?" asked Anna

"In a stall near the hayloft ladder," answered Pam. "We can spy on the whole thing from the hayloft."

"They'll see us," said Anna.

"Not if the hayloft trapdoor is closed," said Pam.

"We can watch the whole thing through the cracks in the floor," explained Lulu. "No one will know we're there."

"We'll hear everything, too," added Pam.

"I'll see Acorn!" exclaimed Anna.

"And in three more days he'll be finished with the movie," Lulu said. "You'll have him back."

Anna felt better. She couldn't wait until tomorrow when she'd see her wonderful pony acting in a movie.

Anna looked out the window at the three ponies at the hitching post. Lightning, Snow White and Daisy stood side by side. Daisy was one of Mrs. Crandal's school ponies! I like

Daisy, thought Anna, but she's not Acorn. She's not my very own pony.

A small van pulled into the diner parking lot. It said, *Wiggins Flowers and Plants* on the side. A woman got out of the truck. She was carrying a huge bouquet of roses.

"Why is she delivering flowers to the diner?" Anna wondered out loud.

"Maybe your father sent flowers to your mother," suggested Lulu. "Is it their anniversary or something?"

"They just had their anniversary," said Anna. "Besides, it's Mom's day off. She's not even here. Dad knows that."

The flower-shop woman came into the restaurant and spoke to the waiter. The waiter turned and pointed to the Pony Pals.

"I think the flowers are for us!" exclaimed Pam.

"Anna Harley?" asked the woman as she came towards the girls.

"That's me," Anna said.

The woman handed Anna the big bouquet of roses.

"I was supposed to leave these here for you," said the woman. "But since you're here I can give them to you personally."

"Thanks," said Anna. "Who sent them?"

The woman pointed to a little card that was attached to the stem of a big pink rose. "It's on the card," she said. Then she turned and left.

"Who sent you flowers?" asked Lulu excitedly. "Read it!"

Anna pulled a small card out of the envelope. "Nobody has ever sent me flowers before," she said.

Anna read the message out loud.

For: Anna Harley

Anna, thank you for letting Acorn act in the movie with me. He's a perfect pony. Yours truly,

Bette Fleming

"Wow!" exclaimed Pam. "Bette sent you flowers!"

"That was so nice of her," added Lulu.

"Yeah," agreed Anna. "It was."

"Maybe she's nicer than we thought," said Lulu.

"You shouldn't judge people just from one meeting," added Pam.

"Bette was probably nervous the day we met her," said Lulu.

"It must be scary to be starting a new movie," added Pam. "And she didn't like Mars, which was a big problem."

"Should we try to be friends with her again?" asked Pam.

"How?" asked Lulu.

"We could invite her for a sleepover," suggested Pam. "She must be sick of being around adults all the time."

"What do you think, Anna?" asked Lulu.

"I don't care," said Anna. "I just want the movie to be over so I can have Acorn back."

Anna smelt the roses. They smelt wonderful and were the most perfect shade of pink.

But why is Bette suddenly being nice to me? Anna wondered.

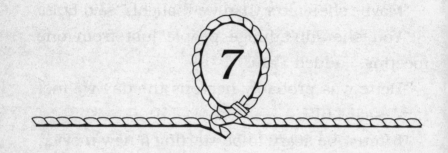

Goodbye Acorn

At six-thirty the next morning Anna and Lulu met in the paddock. Anna did the morning chores while Lulu saddled up Snow White. They were going to the Crandals' to spy on *Megan's Last Ride*.

"The crew is arriving at seven-thirty," Anna reminded Lulu. "We'd better hurry."

Anna put sandwiches, brownies, and boxes of juice in Snow White's saddle bags. "Pam said they're shooting the scene all day, so I brought lots of food," she told Lulu.

By seven-twenty, Snow White was in the Crandals' field with Lightning, and the Pony Pals were in the hayloft with their supplies for the day. Soon they heard trucks on the driveway.

Lulu pushed a haybale over to the hay door. She crouched behind the bale and peeked over it.

Pam and Anna moved a haybale next to Lulu's. From the hay hideout, Anna saw three trucks parked near the barn. Five men and three women unloaded cameras and lights from two of the trucks.

The side of the third truck dropped down to make a counter. "It's a caterer's van," Pam whispered.

In a few minutes the smell of frying bacon reached the hayloft.

Anna heard the crew moving the equipment into the barn. She crawled over to her lookout crack near the trapdoor. She had a perfect view of the crew setting up lights. Pam and Lulu also looked through cracks in the floorboards.

After a while Anna went back to the haybale lookout. She was waiting for a horse trailer to drive up to the barn.

An hour later, four trailers drove in and parked near the trucks. None of them was a horse trailer.

Pam and Lulu joined Anna behind the haybales.

"One of those trailers is for costumes and makeup," Pam whispered. "The others are for the actors. Bette has her own trailer."

"Wow!" exclaimed Anna. "Her own trailer!"

"Sh-sh," warned Pam in a low voice. "They'll hear us."

"Here comes a horse trailer," whispered Lulu. "It must be Acorn."

Anna's heart pounded as Carson led Acorn down the trailer ramp. She was finally seeing her pony.

"Acorn looks great," Pam whispered to Anna.

Anna's eyes filled with tears. Happy tears

because she was seeing her pony; sad tears because she couldn't be with him.

Acorn looked up, sniffed, and whinnied happily.

He loves coming to the Crandals', thought Anna. Just like me.

Lulu leaned closer to Anna. "I think he smells you," she said.

Anna smiled at her friend and nodded. "Maybe," she said as the tears spilled over. Acorn must wonder why I'm not with him, she thought.

Pam elbowed Anna and pointed towards a silver trailer. One of the crew was pushing portable stairs to the door. The door opened and Bette came down the stairs and went over to Acorn.

Acorn whinnied. It sounded like he was saying. "There you are. I'm so happy to see you."

Acorn really likes Bette, thought Anna. This isn't a trick. He isn't acting now.

"Ms. Fleming, please go to costume and makeup," a voice announced over a loudspeaker. Bette gave Acorn a quick hug. She went to the costume trailer and Carson led Acorn towards the Crandals' new barn.

"That's where Carson's grooming him," Pam whispered.

For the next hour the Pony Pals snacked, played checkers, and took turns watching for Acorn.

"Here he comes," Lulu whispered from the haybale lookout.

Anna stretched out and peered through the crack in the floor.

Bette's costume was jeans and a blue T-shirt with a picture of a Shetland pony on it. Ms. Cross was talking to her.

Carson led Acorn into the barn and put him in a stall.

Next, Bette practiced the goodbye scene with Acorn. Anna could hear every word.

"I love you," Bette-as-Megan told Acorn. *"And I'll never forget you."*

Acorn lowered his head sadly.

Megan put her arms around the pony and buried her face in his mane.

"I don't want to leave you," she sobbed. *"I want to stay with you forever. You're my best friend."*

Acorn nickered softly as if to say, "You're my best friend, too."

"Good rehearsal," Ms. Cross said. "Let's shoot it."

Anna noticed that Pam had tears in her eyes. Bette was a terrific actress. So was Acorn.

Bette and Acorn acted the scene over and over again. Sometimes the cameras moved. Sometimes Ms. Cross told Bette to say only one line.

After an hour-and-a half of shooting the scene, someone shouted, "Lunch break. For just an hour, folks."

The cast and crew had their lunch outside.

The Pony Pals had their lunch in the hot, stuffy hayloft.

After lunch, Ms. Cross and the crew came back into the barn. They filmed Acorn alone in the barn, looking very sad.

"Perfect," said Ms. Cross. "Give me a few close-ups of his face. Then he's done."

A few minutes later Carson led Acorn out of the barn and back to the horse trailer.

Anna watched Carson drive away with her pony. She felt sad and lonely. Her pony had been at the Crandals' for five hours and she hadn't even touched him.

After Acorn left, the cameras moved outside. They filmed Bette tearfully walking out of the barn. She got into a car driven by the actor who played Megan's father. The actor playing her mother sat with him in the front seat.

The car drove away.

They shot that scene four times.

Anna was bored. She couldn't wait to leave the hayloft.

Finally, at four o'clock someone shouted. "That's a wrap. Good work, everyone. Thank you."

Pam looked through her crack in the floor. "They're all out of the barn," she told Lulu and Anna. "Let's sneak out. Then we can pretend we just got here."

"We can talk to Bette," suggested Lulu. "I want to see if she'll be nice to us now."

"I should thank her for the flowers," said Anna.

Pam slowly opened the hayloft trapdoor. The girls quickly climbed down and ran outside. They came around the side of the barn.

"Hi," Bette called when she saw them.

The Pony Pals ran over to her.

"Thanks for the flowers," said Anna.

Bette smiled at her. "You're welcome," she said. "Acorn was great today."

"I miss him," said Anna.

"We wondered if you wanted to hang around

with us for a little while," said Pam. "My mother could give you a ride home later."

"I'd love too," said Bette with a big smile. "But I have to go back. I want to ride Acorn this afternoon."

"Let's go, honey," Bette's real mother called from the trailer.

Bette said goodbye and ran to the trailer.

"I didn't know she was riding Acorn all the time," Anna muttered.

Now Anna wished with all her heart that she hadn't let Acorn act in the movie. She missed him too much.

How Much?

"I can't wait to have Acorn back," Anna told Pam and Lulu.

Lulu put an arm around her shoulder. "It's only a little longer," she said.

A man working in the food trailer leaned over the counter. "You girls want a snack before I close the food wagon?" he asked.

A camera operator was eating a cupcake and drinking coffee at the counter. She held up her chocolate cupcake. "These are delicious," she told the girls.

The Pony Pals walked over to the counter. Pam and Lulu took cupcakes. Anna wasn't hungry.

"When will you be finished filming in Wiggins?" Pam asked the camera operator.

"Four more days," the woman answered.

"The pony in the movie is my pony," Anna told the woman. "I can't wait until he's finished."

"He's finished now," said the woman. "Today was his last day."

"He is?" exclaimed Anna. "I didn't know that."

"What about when he runs away and goes to the city?" asked Pam.

"We did those scenes last week," explained the camera woman. She smiled. "He was terrific. He swam across a brook for us, climbed a steep hill and whinnied in front of an apartment building. We don't have any more scenes with him."

"Anna, you'll have Acorn back," said Lulu.

"We can get him tomorrow," added Pam.

"No wonder Bette wanted to ride him this afternoon," said Anna. "It's her last chance."

Anna felt happy again. Her pony was coming home.

That night the Pony Pals had a barn sleepover. Anna woke up with the first morning light. She lay awake thinking about Acorn. I'm not going to wait for Pam and Lulu to wake up, she decided. I'm going to go get Acorn now.

Anna quickly dressed and wrote Pam and Lulu a note.

👁 M PICKING ↑ 🐎

SOON. CU.

♡ ANNA

As Anna walked along the trails to Ms. Wiggins', she remembered riding Acorn there. In a little while she'd be on her pony again, riding this same trail.

When Anna reached Ms. Wiggins', she went right to the house. I'll tell Ms. Cross I'm picking up Acorn, she thought. Then I'll saddle him up and we're out of here.

Bette, her mother, and Ms. Cross were sitting at a table on the porch, eating breakfast.

"Good morning, Anna," Ms. Cross said cheerfully.

Bette and her mother were friendly, too. But Anna could tell they all wondered why she was there.

"I came to pick up Acorn," Anna explained. "Because he's finished his part in the movie."

"You're right," said Ms. Cross. "We *are* finished with him."

Bette looked surprised. "You are?" she said. "Acorn's not going to be in the movie with me anymore?"

"We've finished his scenes, Bette," explained Ms. Cross. "Anna can take him back."

Bette's expression changed from upset to a big smile. A smile for Anna. "Do you want something to eat?" Bette asked.

Anna felt a rumble in her stomach. She hadn't had breakfast and she'd been walking for a long time. There was a platter of pancakes and a bowl of fruit salad on the table.

"Thanks," she said.

Mrs. Fleming handed her an empty dish and the pancakes.

Ms. Cross stood up and said she had to go to work. "We leave for the diner shoot in half-an-hour," she reminded Bette and her mother.

Mrs. Fleming excused herself, too, and left the table.

Bette stayed to keep Anna company. Mostly Bette bragged about being a movie star.

Anna took a last bite of her breakfast. "I'd better get Acorn," she told Bette. "Where is he?"

"I'll show you," said Bette.

The two girls walked to the field.

"I love Acorn," Bette told Anna. "It was so

much fun to pretend I had my own pony. I was going to ride him after work today."

The two girls turned the corner of the barn and faced the paddock. Acorn and Ms. Wiggins' black horse, Picasso, were grazing together.

"Acorn!" called Bette as she and Anna went into the field.

Acorn ran towards them. Bette put out her arms and Acorn nuzzled her shoulder. She wrapped her arms around him in a big hug. When Bette finished hugging Acorn, she gave him a signal to bow. He bowed to Bette, then turned and trotted back to Picasso.

Acorn didn't even look at me, thought Anna. Tears came to her eyes.

"He is such a great pony!" said Bette. "Anna, please can't he stay one more day? That way I can have one last ride. You can get him tomorrow."

Anna felt a knot in her throat. It felt like Acorn didn't know her. Anna didn't want to cry in front of Bette. She swallowed hard, looked at the ground and said, "Okay."

Bette jumped up and down with happiness. "Thank you, thank you," she shouted.

Mrs. Fleming came up to them. "What's all the excitement?" she asked.

Bette told her mother that Acorn was staying for another day.

"Great," said Mrs. Fleming. "Bette has to go to her trailer now, but why don't I give you a ride home, Anna."

"I stayed over at the Crandals'," Anna said. "Where you were yesterday."

"I'm happy to drive you there," said Mrs. Fleming. "After all, you're being so sweet to Bette."

Anna took a last look at Acorn. He was facing the other way. It didn't even feel like he was her pony anymore.

9

Are You My Pony?

Anna sat next to Mrs. Fleming in the car.

"You seem like a sweet girl, Anna," Mrs. Fleming said as they drove towards town. "And generous. That was so nice of you to let Acorn stay with us."

"Just for today," Anna reminded Mrs. Fleming.

"That's what I want to talk to you about," said Mrs. Fleming. She smiled at Anna. "Bette's birthday is next week. I asked her what she'd like for a present, and guess what she answered? *Mom,* she said. *More than anything in the world, I want Acorn.*"

"He's *my* pony," Anna said, horrified.

"I'd like to buy him from you, Anna," said Mrs. Fleming.

Anna couldn't believe her ears. Bette and her mother thought she'd sell Acorn!

"He's not for sale," Anna told her.

"Bette and Acorn have such a special relationship," said Mrs. Fleming. "So I'll pay *a lot* of money for him. That way you can buy another pony—a very special pony. Or maybe a horse. Wouldn't that be exciting?"

Anna knew that if she tried to talk she'd cry. She didn't want to cry in front of Mrs. Fleming. She needed her Pony Pals.

Mrs. Fleming pulled into the Crandals' driveway and stopped the car. She put a hand on Anna's shoulder.

"You don't have to decide today, dear," Mrs. Fleming said. "Think it over and talk to your parents. Tell them I'm ready to pay a very good price for Acorn."

Anna opened the car door. "Thank you for the ride," she said as she got out of the car.

"Remember, Anna," Mrs. Fleming said, "you can name the price."

Anna turned and ran up the driveway. Tears streamed down her face.

Pam and Lulu were in the field with their ponies. Anna ran up to them.

"What's wrong?" asked Lulu.

"Where's Acorn?" asked Pam. "Do they still need him for the movie?"

"Bette wants her mother to buy Acorn," sobbed Anna.

"You told her no, didn't you?" said Pam.

"I tried," Anna told them. "But Mrs. Fleming said I should think about it . . . until tomorrow."

"You're not going to sell Acorn!" exclaimed Lulu. "Why would you?"

"He . . . he," stammered Anna through her tears. "He loves Bette more than me."

Lulu put an arm around Anna's shoulder.

"Anna, tell us what happened," said Pam softly.

Anna told Pam and Lulu about seeing Acorn with Bette and then the car ride with Mrs. Fleming.

"Acorn might like Bette," said Lulu, "because he's been with her in the movie. But that doesn't mean he likes her better than you."

"But he came right over to her," Anna said. "And ignored me."

"They've trained him to act like that," said Pam. "Bette probably gave him lots of treats."

"Acorn didn't know it made *you* feel bad," added Lulu. "He probably thought he was being a good pony."

"So I don't have to sell Acorn to Bette," said Anna.

"No!" exclaimed Lulu and Pam together.

"Let's go and tell Mrs. Fleming that she can't buy Acorn," added Pam. "Not for *any* price."

"Bette thinks she can have anything she wants," said Lulu.

"Because she's a big deal movie star," added Pam. "But she can't have Acorn."

"They're shooting at the diner today," Anna told her friends.

The Pony Pals half-walked, half-ran to the diner.

Trailers were lined up on Belgo Road. Men and women from the film crew were setting up their lights and cameras. People from Wiggins were standing around watching.

"They probably want to see Bette," said Pam.

"I wonder where she is," said Lulu.

Just then, Anna spotted Bette and her mother coming out of one of the trailers.

The Pony Pals ran over to them.

"Hello," said Mrs. Fleming cheerfully. "Do you have some good news for us, Anna?"

"When Acorn's mine I'll tell the whole world,"

said Bette proudly. "His picture would be in the paper with me all the time."

Anna wasn't upset any more. She was angry. Bette thought she could have Acorn just because she wanted him!

"Acorn is *my* pony," said Anna. "I won't sell him for any price. That's what I came to tell you."

Bette's eyes filled with tears. "But I love Acorn," she cried.

"So do I!" exclaimed Anna.

"Don't cry, Bette," her mother scolded. "You'll ruin your makeup."

Bette ignored her mother. She glared at Anna. "I *want Acorn!*" Bette insisted. "You *have* to sell him to me."

Anna put her hands on her hips. "No, I don't!" she said.

A man with a walkie-talkie came up to them. "Ms. Fleming, we need you on the diner steps," he told Bette.

Bette turned to Anna. "Then can I have one last ride on Acorn?" she asked. "Just one."

"No!" said Anna.

Anna watched Bette walk towards the diner.

A woman with a powder puff and a man carrying a hairbrush and hair spray followed them over to the car.

"Will you come with me to get Acorn?" Anna asked her friends.

"Sure," said Pam.

"But let's watch for a minute first," added Lulu.

Bette was standing near the diner steps with the other actors. The hairdresser was combing her hair. The makeup artist was powdering her face.

One of the bystanders yelled, "We love you, Bette!"

"She has sort of a weird life," said Pam. "Everyone spoils her."

"Do you think I should have let her ride Acorn one more time?" Anna asked her friends.

"It's up to you, Anna," said Pam. "He's your pony."

"I guess she wants to say goodbye to him," said Anna.

"Maybe it'd be okay if we all rode together," suggested Lulu.

"And I could ride Daisy," added Anna. "After that, Acorn will be mine forever and ever."

I want Acorn back with all my heart, thought Anna. But what if he doesn't want to be with me?

Sleepover

The Pony Pals motioned to Bette that they wanted to talk to her.

She ran over to them.

"Did you change your mind?" Bette asked Anna. "Will you sell Acorn to me. Please say yes."

"No," Anna told her. "I won't change my mind."

Bette frowned.

"Do you want to go on a trail ride with us later?" Lulu asked Bette.

"I'll ride Daisy," said Anna. "So you can ride Acorn one more time."

Bette's frown turned into a sad smile. "I'd like that," she said. "I didn't think I'd ever see him again. Now I can say goodbye."

"That's what I thought," said Anna.

"I have to go," Bette told the Pony Pals. "But I'll be finished at five o'clock."

"We'll meet you at Ms. Wiggins'," Pam told her.

Bette turned and ran back to work. Suddenly she stopped and turned around. She waved and yelled, "Thanks. See you later."

Lulu and Pam waved back.

"Maybe she's nice after all," said Lulu.

"I don't think so," said Anna.

The Pony Pals rode up to Ms. Wiggins' barn at five sharp.

Bette led Acorn out of the barn. He was saddled and ready for a trail ride.

"Hi," said Bette as she mounted Acorn.

"Where would you like to ride?" asked Lulu.

"Where do you ride to get here?" asked Bette. "Can we go on those trails?"

"We came from Pam's house," said Lulu.

"Let's go there," said Bette. "Okay?"

"Sure," agreed Pam as she turned Lightning around.

Anna noticed that Acorn was looking at her. She smiled and said his name. He nodded, looked back at Bette, then back to Anna. To Anna, he seemed confused. The four girls rode side by side across Ms. Wiggins' field.

"Will you show me where you have your barn sleepovers and everything?" asked Bette.

"Okay," said Pam.

"We're having one tonight," added Lulu. "In the hayloft."

"That must be so much fun," Bette said. "I never do anything like that."

The Pony Pals exchanged a glance. Lulu nodded. Anna shrugged her shoulders.

"You can sleep over too," Pam told Bette. "If you want."

"I can?" Bette said. "Wow! Thanks. That'd be so great."

Anna couldn't wait for the trail ride to be over. Then, finally, Acorn would be her pony again . . . if he still loved her.

They reached the beginning of the trail.

"Okay," Anna said. "Let's go. Pam, it's your turn to be first. I'll go next."

"Bette, you go after Anna," said Lulu. "I'll take up the rear."

The four girls rode single file along the trail.

"Stay in line," Anna heard Bette tell Acorn.

When the trail grew wider, Acorn suddenly burst ahead and trotted beside Daisy.

"He's been trying to pull ahead the whole time," Bette told Anna.

Acorn whinnied and pushed at Daisy with his head.

"Acorn," scolded Bette. "Behave."

Acorn moved in front of Daisy, stopped, and blocked her way.

"Acorn's up to his old tricks," said Anna.

Pam turned Lightning around. "What's going on?" she asked.

"He's never acted like this before," said Bette.

"I think he's jealous," said Lulu. "Acorn doesn't want Anna on another pony."

Acorn pushed Daisy with his head again.

"That must be it," said Pam.

Anna couldn't help smiling as she backed Daisy away from Acorn. She felt so happy. Acorn is jealous of Daisy, she thought. He wants me to ride him. Acorn was still her pony.

"Maybe Daisy and I should be last," suggested Anna. "So Acorn can't see me."

"He wants you," said Bette as she slid off Acorn. "He's your pony. You should ride him."

"Okay," Anna agreed as she quickly jumped off Daisy. Acorn nudged Anna with his nose. She hugged him.

Acorn whinnied happily as if to say, "I missed you!"

"I missed you, too," Anna whispered in his ear.

Bette mounted Daisy and Anna mounted Acorn.

86

"Are you all right riding Daisy?" Anna asked Bette.

Bette had tears in her eyes, but she smiled. "Of course, I am," she said. "I'm a very good rider."

"You had a lot of trouble riding Mars," commented Lulu.

"That was acting," laughed Bette. "I pretended I couldn't ride Mars, because I wanted Acorn to star in the movie with me." She leaned over and patted Acorn's head. "And I'm glad he did."

Acorn nickered softly.

"Anna, you and Acorn take the lead now," said Pam.

Anna pulled Acorn out in front and gave her pony the signal to go.

As they galloped along the trails, Anna's heart soared. She felt the heat of her pony's body under her and the cool wind on her face.

She and Acorn were partners again. He was her pony. And he always would be.

It was the best ride of her life.

Dear Pony Pal:

There are now Pony Pals all over the United States, Australia, New Zealand, Canada, Germany and Norway.

When I first started writing the Pony Pals I thought there would only be six books. Now there are twenty-six books. I am surprised that I have so many stories to tell about Pam, Anna, Lulu and their ponies. They are like real people, who keep having adventures that I want to write down for them.

When I am not writing Pony Pal or CHEER USA books, I like to swim, hike, draw and paint. I also like to visit horse farms and talk to people who love and ride ponies and horses. I don't ride anymore and have never owned my own pony or horse. But my husband and I have two young cats, Lucca and Todi. They are brothers and get along great with our old dog, Willie.

It's wonderful to know that so many Pony Pals from different parts of the world enjoy the adventures of Pam, Anna, Lulu, Lightning, Acorn and Snow White. I think about you when I am writing. A special thankyou to those who have written me letters and sent drawings and photos. I love your drawings of ponies and keep your photos on the wall near my computer. They inspire me to write more Pony Pal stories.

Remember, you don't need a pony to be a Pony Pal.

Happy Reading,

Jeanne Betancourt